W9-CMB-267

BEEBEAR ™

by Ross C. Follett • Illustrated by Lee Sievers

OddInt Media

First Printing 2013

ISBN 978-0-9881748-5-6

Dear Reader,

I hope you like this book. It is a good size to be in small hands and on bedroom floors. Its words are fun to talk about. Its pictures are great to look at. You could point at the bee. I'm glad you have this book.

Ross C. Follett

BEEBEAR™

Dedicated to

Children and adults
reading to each other

FRIENDS

A bee met a bear
At a grocery store

The bear wanted honey
But didn't have money

The bee had honey
But didn't want money

They talked through and traded
Those means and those ends

And ever since then
Have been very close friends

DRIVE

Happy being alive
The bee and the bear took a drive

They didn't know where they were going
And didn't care when they'd arrive

FLOWERS

The bee and the bear
Like flowers

They could sit and watch
Flowers for hours

They love the way
Wild flowers look

And have yet
To press one in a book

LOST

The bee got lost
In the bear's hair

The bear found it

LOOKOUT

The bear and the bee
Went to sea

The bear was the lookout
And the bee rowed

HARDER

The bee and the bear
Went up a tree

It was harder for the bear
Than it was for the bee

SMALL

Of the bee and the bear
Which has more hair
If you look in just
A very small square

FAR

The bee and the bear
Got in the car

It was out of gas
But they weren't going far

MOVIE

There at the movie
The bear saw the show

For the bee however
The seats were too low

JUMPED

The bear and the bee
Jumped out of a tree

The bear hit the ground
The bee messed around

DINNER

The bee and the bear
Went out to dinner

Where the bear got fatter
But the bee got thinner

BIGGER

The bear is bigger
Than the bee

But not compared
To the sea

BOXED

The bee and the bear
Stood and boxed

The bear beat the air
The bee below the knee

The thing went all 15 rounds

LISTEN

All the while
They listen to music
The bear and the bee
Both smile

ROCKED

The bee and the bear
Went to the fair
And rode on the Ferris Wheel there

They made quite a pair
But the bear had a scare
When the bee rocked the Ferris Wheel chair

TRAVEL

The bear and the bee travel light

The bear takes a comb
And that's all

The bee has a suitcase
But it's small

CHAIR

The bee and the bear
Bought a chair

For the bear to sit in
When the bee wasn't there

RACED

The bee and the bear raced

The bee standing
On the bear's head
And leaning forward

Barely won

SNIFF

The bear wrote a poem
And the bee read it

About a bee and a bear
And how they would dread it

If either were neither
And the other hadn't said it

WATCH

Sometimes the bear
Wanted to be like the bee

And sometimes the bee
Like the bear

They thought however
Since they could watch each other

With such envy
Really neither should bother

THUMPA

The music they made
Was hardly ho-hum
When the bee buzzed
And the bear beat the drum

WALK

The bear and the bee
Took a walk
To just look around
And talk